The School is ALIVE!

By Jack Chabert
Illustrated by Sam Ricks

SCHOLASTIC INC.

READ ALL ABOUT
Eerie Elementary!

Table of Contents

To the greatest hall monitor in the history of hall monitors, Matthew McArdle — JC

Library of Congress Cataloging-in-Publication Data

Chabert, Jack, author.
The school is alive! / by Jack Chabert ; illustrated by Sam Ricks.
pages cm. — (Eerie Elementary ; 1)
Summary: Sam Graves discovers that his elementary school is alive and plotting against the students, and, as hall monitor, it is his job to protect them — but he will need some help from his friends.
ISBN 978-0-545-62392-6 (pbk.) — ISBN 978-0-545-62393-3 (hardcover) — ISBN 978-0-545-62394-0 (ebook) 1. Elementary schools — Juvenile fiction. 2. Best friends—Juvenile fiction. 3. Horror tales. [1. Schools — Fiction. 2. Best friends — Fiction. 3. Friendship — Fiction. 4. Horror stories.] I. Ricks, Sam, illustrator. II. Title.
PZ7.C3313Sc 2014
813.6 — dc23
2013034498

ISBN 978-0-545-62393-3 (hardcover) / ISBN 978-0-545-62392-6 (paperback)

10 9 8 7 6 5 4 3 2 1 14 15 16 17 18 19/0

Printed in South China 38

First Scholastic printing, July 2014
Book design by Will Denton
Edited by Katie Carella

IT BEGINS . . .

1

"This is HORRIBLE!" said Sam Graves. He was holding up a shiny orange sash. "I can't *believe* I have to wear this."

It was Monday morning, and Sam and his best friends Antonio and Lucy were standing in front of their lockers. They were waiting for the bell to ring.

"Wait, you're a hall monitor?!" Antonio said. "I didn't even know Eerie Elementary *had* hall monitors."

Sam kicked at the floor. "They do now. And it stinks! The principal called my mom last night and said I had been chosen. *Ugh*. It's going to be *terrible*. I have to stand in the hallway and yell 'Get to class!' and 'No skateboarding!'"

"Well, at least you get to wear that cool orange sash," Lucy teased.

Sam stuck out his tongue.

RIIIIING!!

"Come on, that's the bell!" Antonio said.

Sam frowned. "You guys go ahead. I have to make sure everyone has gone into class."

"We'll see you inside!" Lucy shouted.

Within moments, the hallway was totally empty. Totally empty, except for Sam.

He began walking the halls. Sam looked through the double doors to the outside. He saw a classmate by the playground.

"Hey, Bryan!" Sam called out. "The bell rang. You should . . . um . . . get to class!" Bryan frowned at Sam. Then he ran past him into the school.

See? Everyone hates the hall monitor, thought Sam. He was about to close the door when a cold breeze blew past. He saw that Bryan had dropped his hat near the playground.

My teacher won't mind if I sneak outside for a second, thought Sam.

The air outside was like ice. Orange and red leaves whipped across the ground. Sam shoved his hands into his pockets. He could see his breath. It looked like little ghosts were dancing through the air in front of him.

Sam looked up at the school building. He thought it looked like an old castle made of crumbling, red brick. The paint on the doors and windows was chipped. Big, black crows sat on the roof, watching Sam. The whole thing gave him the willies.

Sam didn't want to be out there any longer than he had to. He ran over to the playground. He was near the swings when something grabbed his ankle.

Sam looked down. His feet were sinking into the sand!

Now, of course, feet *do* sink into sand. But not like this! Something was pulling him under.

"HELP!" Sam shouted.

The sand was up above his sneakers. He reached down to try to pull his feet free. The sand was wet!

Quicksand?!

This was just like the quicksand from the old *Tarzan* movies Sam's dad made him watch. But Sam was pretty sure that quicksand was found in jungles in the movies, not on real-life playgrounds!

"Help! The playground is *eating me*!" Sam shouted.

The sand was up to his knees now. Sam fought and kicked. He watched as Bryan's hat was swallowed up by the sand.

It was no use.

The cold, wet sand was up to his waist.

Sam squeezed his eyes shut as he was pulled down, deeper and deeper. . . .

MR. NEKOBI

2

Just as the quicksand was about to swallow Sam, a hand grabbed his wrist! His eyes shot open. It was Mr. Nekobi, the old man who took care of the school.

Mr. Nekobi tugged. Sam was yanked free.

Sam gasped for air. "The playground sand," Sam said. "It just tried to eat me!"

Mr. Nekobi slowly got to his feet. He was out of breath, too. His face looked like a piece of paper that someone had balled up and then tried to flatten again. He stared at Sam. His eyes were small and gray. A chill went up Sam's spine.

Mr. Nekobi growled, "You should be more careful. Or you won't last long as hall monitor, Sam Graves."

"Be careful of what? Be careful because other parts of the school might try to eat me?!" Sam said. Then he paused. "Wait — what does my being the hall monitor have to do with this? And why do *you* care if I stay on as hall monitor or not?"

Mr. Nekobi began walking away. Over his shoulder, he said, "Because I'm the one who chose you."

"What does that mean?" Sam asked.

But Mr. Nekobi didn't answer. He simply turned the corner, out of sight.

Sam shook his head, thinking, *This has been the weirdest day of my life! And it's only 8:30 in the morning!*

He needed to tell Lucy and Antonio about the quicksand and about creepy Mr. Nekobi. But first he had to ditch the orange sash. Sam darted inside and flung open his locker.

Whoa!

He stumbled back and threw his hand over his nose. His locker stunk!

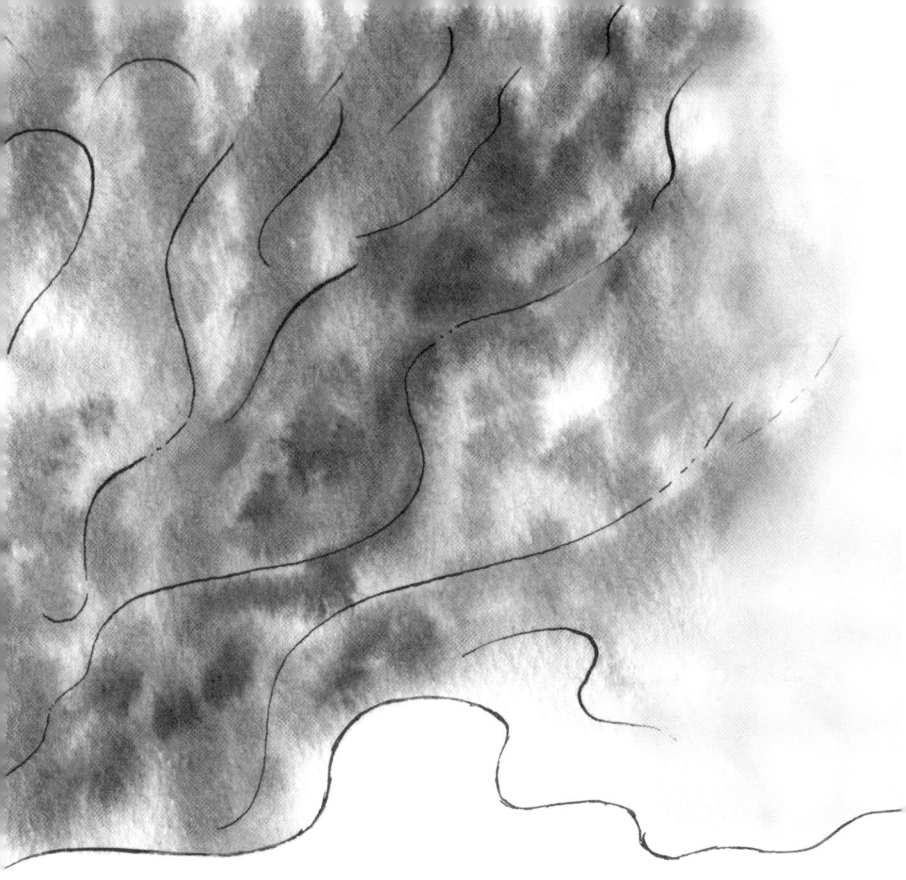

The smell coming out of Sam's locker reminded him of rotten chocolate milk or something. "Yikes, what did I leave in here?" he asked.

Sam shoved the sash inside his locker. Then he knew what it smelled like: *really* bad breath.

TICKTOCK, TICKTOCK

3

Sam slammed his locker shut. He rushed into Ms. Grinker's classroom. Ms. Grinker was short and thin, with frizzy gray hair. She was listing everyone's parts for Friday's class play on the board.

Sam slid into his desk between Antonio and Lucy. He whispered, "Guys, the freakiest thing just happened. I got trapped in *quicksand* on the playground!"

Lucy scrunched up her forehead. Antonio scratched his chin. Then they both tried not to laugh.

"If it happened to you," Sam whispered, "you wouldn't be laughing."

"Sam! Lucy! Antonio!" yelled Ms. Grinker.

All three kids faced front.

"Please pay attention," Ms. Grinker said. "I am still giving out the parts for *Peter Pan*."

"I'm playing Peter Pan!" Antonio whispered to Sam. He had a big smile on his face. He always did. He was the happiest kid Sam knew.

"And I'm playing Wendy," Lucy whispered.

"Sam Graves, you'll be playing Noodler. He is one of Captain Hook's friendly pirates," said Ms. Grinker. Sam nodded but all he could think about was the man-eating playground.

As the day wound down, Sam stared out the window. An old oak tree was blowing in the breeze. It was moving strangely. Sam leaned forward on his desk. The tree looked like a giant oak hand, waving at Sam.

Sam shivered. Then he looked at the clock across the room. *How long until this day is over?* he thought.

Sam could hear the clock:

How can I hear the clock from all the way over here? he wondered.

Then the sound of the clock changed. Sam no longer heard *ticktock*, *ticktock*, *ticktock*. The sound became *Ba BUMP . . . Ba BUMP . . .*

Sam was even more confused. *That doesn't sound like a normal clock. But I* do *know that sound. . . .*

Ba BUMP, Ba BUMP, Ba BUMP.
Ba BUMP, Ba BUMP, Ba BUMP.

It sounded like a beating heart!

SOMETHING AWAKENS

4

Sam covered his ears. But he couldn't get away from the sound of the clock. Not until—

RING!

The day was over. Sam followed the other kids into the hall. He grabbed the hall monitor sash from his stinky locker.

"See you tomorrow, Sam!" Lucy said. She and Antonio threw their backpacks over their shoulders and ran outside.

Sam sighed. He wanted to run home, too. He wanted to plop down on the couch and fall asleep. Then he wanted to wake up to learn this whole day had been a terrible nightmare. But instead he had to go on hall monitor duty.

Sam stood near the third-grade lockers. The only thing keeping Sam awake was the cool chill across his neck. It felt like the school was breathing on him. Sam saw that he was beneath an air vent.

Brrrr!

There were no teachers around. So Sam thought there'd be no harm in sitting down. He slipped into a chair just outside the principal's office. *I'll only rest here for a minute. . . .*

But soon Sam's eyelids felt heavy. They were closing. Sam was falling asleep.

When Sam woke up, he was *beyond* confused. The halls were dark—nearly pitch-black.

What time is it? he wondered, standing up.

Sam rubbed his eyes. He ran to the end of the hall. He peered through the big double doors. It was black as midnight outside.

How long was I asleep? My mom is going to freak out, thought Sam. *I have to get home now!*

He yanked on the doors, but they were locked.

"Hello?" Sam whispered. "Is anyone here? I fell asleep and—"

CLANG! CLANG! CLANG!

Sam spun around. All of the locker doors flung open, one after the other, all the way down the hall!

Sam jumped back. His heart was pounding.

CLANG!

CLANG!

CLANG!

All the locker doors slammed shut again! Sam was really hoping this was just a nightmare! He spun back around. He tugged as hard as he could on the doors.

But it was no use.

He was trapped.

Trapped inside Eerie Elementary.

THE SKELETON

5

The double doors flew open, knocking Sam to the floor. Then they slammed shut again. He was still trapped inside the school. "Ouch!" Sam yelled. *Everyone knows you can't get hurt in a dream, so this must be real!*

He needed to escape! The school was coming to life all around him!

Sam ran into his classroom. He threw his hands against the large window. He was hoping to see someone, anyone, who could help him.

All he saw was the giant oak tree blowing in the wind.

But it *wasn't* windy. Sam saw other trees and none of those trees were blowing. And the leaves on the ground weren't whooshing around at all. The only thing moving was that tree!

Could the tree be alive? Sam thought.

SMASH!!

The glass window shattered. Sam fell to the floor as one of the tree's long, twisted branches came crashing through. It wrapped around Sam's leg.

Sam began hitting the branch.

Whack! Whack! Whack!

Finally, the branch's grip loosened. Sam was able to crawl away. Behind him, he heard the branch scraping across the floor like fingernails on a chalkboard. The tree was reaching for him, trying to pull him back.

He pushed his way through fallen desks. He stumbled back into the hallway. Pieces of glass crunched beneath his feet. Then —

CLANG! CLANG! CLANG!

All the locker doors were slamming open and shut at once. All the classroom doors were doing the same thing.

But worst of all was what Sam saw next: A figure stood at the end of the hallway. It had a body like a skeleton.

Lights flashed and doors clanged. But the figure didn't move. It just stood there, perfectly still, staring at Sam.

6
THE DANGER IS REAL

All of the sudden, the figure started running toward Sam. It was Mr. Nekobi!

"What's happening?!" Sam shouted.

"No time to explain! Get down!" Mr. Nekobi yelled.

One of the hallway fire hoses had come to life!

It was like a long octopus tentacle. The hose crashed into the old man and knocked him to the floor. Then it came for Sam.

Sam ducked as the fire hose whipped above his head. **BLAM!**

The heavy metal nozzle slammed into the lockers.

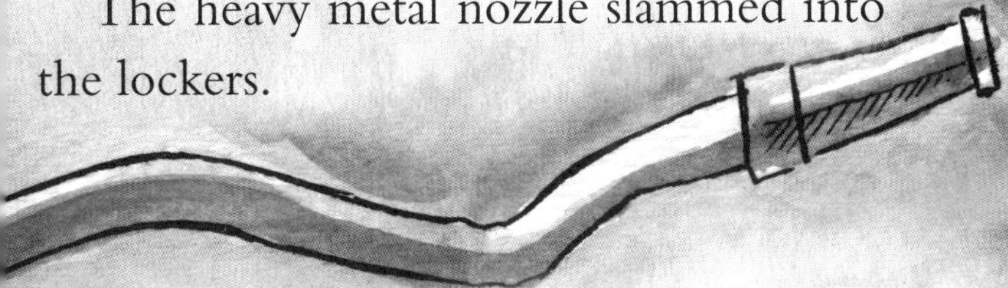

"That thing almost hit me!" Sam gasped.

The fire hose wasn't done. It kept whipping through the air.

"Wrestle it!" Mr. Nekobi shouted.

"ARE YOU NUTS?!" Sam screamed.

"Grab on to it!" Mr. Nekobi yelled from down on the floor.

Sam gulped. The fire hose whipped around again. Sam leapt up in the air just as the hose flew beneath him. He wrapped both his arms around it and held on tight.

"*AHHH!*" he screamed.

"Tie the hose!" Mr. Nekobi yelled.

Sam grabbed the hose and tugged. He used all his might to pull the hose back around itself. He knotted it like a giant shoelace. The monstrous fire hose shook. It was choking!

The hose crashed to the ground.

WHOOMP! Sam smacked against the cold hallway floor.

And just like that, everything stopped: the wild fire hose, the banging lockers, and the flashing lights.

"The school hasn't been this active in a very long time. . . ." Mr. Nekobi said, getting to his feet.

Sam blinked twice. "Um, what?"

"Never mind. It's late. You should go home."

"But the school, it's — it's alive?!" Sam said. "I don't understand —"

Mr. Nekobi handed Sam his backpack. "Get home. Now," he ordered.

Sam wanted answers. But even more than answers, he wanted *out of that school.* He turned on his heels, shoved open the now unlocked double doors, and ran home. He didn't stop once.

"Where have you been?!" Sam's mom yelled as Sam came running through the door. "I was worried sick."

Sam threw his backpack onto the kitchen floor. He kicked off his sneakers. One nearly hit his mom in the head. The other bounced off a cabinet. "Mom, you wouldn't believe it!" Sam said. In between gulping for air, he began to tell the tale: "First, I almost got eaten by quicksand! Then a tree broke through the classroom window and —"

"Sam," his mom said, cutting him off, "tell me the *real* reason you are late."

Sam sighed. Of course she wasn't going to believe him. Antonio and Lucy had not believed him, either.

At last, Sam said, "Hall monitor duty."

BELIEVE ME!

7

"I, Peter Pan, challenge the friendly pirate Noodler to a fight!" Antonio yelled. He swung an invisible sword through the air.

It was Tuesday morning, and Sam, Antonio, and Lucy were walking to school. They were practicing their *Peter Pan* lines.

But Sam couldn't focus on his lines. He could not stop thinking about what had happened the night before.

Antonio laughed. "Sam, you have the worst part in the play. You only have a few lines toward the end. And, really, who wants to be a *friendly* pirate anyway?"

"Huh?" Sam said.

"Sam's not even paying attention!" Lucy moaned. "This play is going to be a disaster. Everything is going to go wrong!"

Antonio patted his pocket, smiling. "Not as long as I have my lucky sandwich." Antonio and Sam had been friends since kindergarten. And Antonio had always carried a peanut butter and jelly sandwich around in his pocket.

Sometimes he carried the same sandwich around for weeks. Sam thought it was a little bit disgusting but also a little bit awesome.

Sam stopped walking. "Guys, I really need to tell you something."

Sam looked around to make sure no one was nearby. He pulled his friends in close.

"Remember the quicksand I told you about yesterday? I know you didn't believe me. But after school, *more* weird stuff happened! I fell asleep while on hall monitor duty —"

"I believe that!" Antonio joked.

"Listen!" Sam said. "When I woke up, the school was going crazy! I was attacked by the oak tree! Then Mr. Nekobi saved me! But I think he might be a bad guy or something — he's super weird!"

Antonio frowned. "You're losing your mind."

Lucy agreed. "I'm starting to worry about you, Sam."

Sam ran his hand through his hair and said, "Just wait until we get to school. You'll see! There's a broken window and busted lockers! And the fire hose is tied in a big knot!"

When they got to school, Sam rushed past his friends and up the front steps.

What he saw blew his mind.

Everything was back to normal! It was like nothing had happened. The fire hose was wound up, and the lockers were closed.

"No . . ." Sam whispered. "This doesn't make any sense. . . ."

Antonio gently punched Sam in the arm. "You should really get some more sleep. Your nightmares sound *serious*."

RIIIIING!

The morning bell rang, and everyone began filing into class. The huge window in Ms. Grinker's class wasn't broken. Even the oak tree looked normal.

This was a regular Tuesday morning.

But not for Sam.

Sam wanted answers, and he thought he knew where to get them. But first —

"Sam, hurry up!" Lucy said, running into class.

Sam groaned. He had to check the halls and then get to class, too. His answers would have to wait.

8
INTO THE DARKNESS

As soon as the bell rang for recess, Sam went looking for Mr. Nekobi.

He spotted him outside the janitor's closet. Sam watched Mr. Nekobi open the closet door. Mr. Nekobi looked both ways down the hall, like he was afraid he was being watched. Then, very slowly, the old man reached into the dark closet. He grabbed hold of a dim, swinging light bulb. Mr. Nekobi tugged twice on the light bulb.

BRUMMMMMMMM! There was a low rumbling noise as the rear wall of the closet began to move.

A secret door! Sam thought.

Mr. Nekobi stepped through.

Sam swallowed. Sweat was pouring off his brow. He needed to know the truth about Eerie Elementary. This was his chance.

Sam darted across the hall. He closed the closet door behind him. Then he leapt through the secret doorway.

Sam found himself in a large room with punching bags, pieces of old lockers, and school chairs with three legs. The room was dark. It smelled wet.

"Sam Graves," Mr. Nekobi said. "I've been waiting for —"

Sam cut him off. "What happened last night? And how is everything back to normal today? I *know* I didn't imagine all that stuff!"

Mr. Nekobi said, "You imagined nothing. Place your hand against the wall, Sam, and *focus*."

Sam frowned. "You're nuts."

"Do you want to know the truth or not?" Mr. Nekobi said.

Sam sighed, then placed his palm against the cool brick wall. The room grew quiet.

Then, he heard it: the soft sound of air blowing. And he felt it: The wall was gently swaying.

It was the school. *The school* was breathing.

Sam backed away from the wall. "Wh-what's happening?" he stuttered.

Mr. Nekobi walked toward Sam. As his face passed through the shadows, he looked almost inhuman. "Eerie Elementary is . . . alive," Mr. Nekobi said.

Sam shook his head. "That can't be. That's impossible!"

Mr. Nekobi continued, "This school is a living, breathing thing. It is a beast. A monster. And there is only one person who can keep its students safe."

"Who?" Sam asked softly.

Mr. Nekobi stooped down until he was face-to-face with Sam. "*You*, Sam Graves — the hall monitor."

HERO?

In a strange, hidden room, this man was telling Sam that the school was *alive*? And that *he* was supposed to keep everyone safe? He couldn't believe it.

"I, too, was a hall monitor," said Mr. Nekobi. "Eerie Elementary's *first* hall monitor. And since then, I have been here to fight the school and protect the students. But now I am old and weak. And the school *knows* it. The school knows that *now* is the time to strike. It is planning something big."

Sam collapsed in a chair. There were goose bumps all over his body. "But how can the school be alive? I don't understand."

"The source of the school's power is a mystery," Mr. Nekobi said. "But I know this: *It is evil.* It feeds on students, and it has not fed in a long time. It is hungry. . . ."

Sam's heart was pounding.

Mr. Nekobi continued, "As hall monitor,

you have the ability to *sense* the school — to see and feel and hear what others cannot. But you must be careful, because the school can sense you, too. It has attacked you twice already. It knows you are its enemy."

Sam gulped.

Mr. Nekobi said softly, "You must be our hero now, Sam Graves."

Do I have it in me? Sam wondered.

Sam thought about the quicksand and the trec and the lockers. *What if that had happened to Lucy or Antonio? The school could have eaten them! And if the school is planning something big, then my friends are in danger. . . .*

Sam turned to Mr. Nekobi and said, "Okay. I'll do what I must."

Mr. Nekobi smiled. "Good."

"So now what?" asked Sam.

"Now you begin your training," said Mr. Nekobi. He yanked on a filthy white sheet, uncovering what looked to be a large metal monster. Then he walked back out through the secret door, leaving Sam all alone — or so he thought.

The giant metal thing was made up of different parts: an old refrigerator, pieces of a vending machine, and banged-up lockers. It had a rusty head dotted with two splashes of red paint. There were brooms, buckets, and wooden hockey sticks jutting out from it, too.

Sam took a deep breath. He was about to step toward it, when —

"Sam!" a voice shouted.

Sam spun around. It was Antonio!

"Antonio! What are you doing here?" Sam exclaimed.

"I followed you, since you've been acting like a total weirdo. I was hiding behind some junk over there," Antonio said.

"Did you — did you hear everything Mr. Nekobi said?" Sam asked.

Antonio nodded.

"Do you believe him?" Sam asked.

"Not really. I think you're both crazy," said Antonio. Then he walked over to the machine. There was a note taped to the front. Antonio tore it off.

Antonio smiled and said, "I may not believe you, but I will help you train. This big monster machine-thing is awesome!"

Sam perked up. Having a friend by his side made him feel 1,000 times better.

"Look, there's a switch on the front," Antonio said. He flicked the switch and the machine came to life.

Antonio jumped back. The giant machine charged toward Sam. The top part spun, and a hockey stick lashed out. Sam rolled underneath the hockey stick. He came up behind the machine. The machine's head whirled around. It began shooting tennis balls out of its big, round eyes!

“Watch out!” Antonio said.

Sam threw his arm over his face, but the tennis balls knocked him to the ground.

Sam pounded his fists on the cement floor. "This is ridiculous! I don't know how to do any of this!" he yelled.

Antonio stuck out his hand, quickly helping his friend to his feet. "Try using what's around you."

VAA-SHOOOOM!!

A tennis ball whizzed between Sam and Antonio. Antonio dove behind a nearby trash can. Sam looked around and saw a busted locker door.

Here goes nothing, he thought. Sam grabbed the locker door, held it up like a shield, and ran straight at the machine. The tennis balls bounced off it.

When Sam got close enough, he tossed the door aside and climbed on top of the machine. Then he yanked the electrical cord from its head.

The machine rumbled and coughed. Finally, it went silent.

Sam hopped down.

"Wow," Antonio said, scratching the back of his neck. "Dude, you're kind of awesome right now!"

Sam turned to his friend, smiling. "But it sounds like this was only the beginning."

SOMETHING BIG

11

For the next two days, Sam and Antonio trained before school, during recess, and after school. Lucy now thought *both* of her best friends were losing their minds. She wouldn't believe a word they said.

Sometimes Mr. Nekobi poked his head in to check on Sam, but the old man didn't do much else. Sam understood that Mr. Nekobi was weak. Now it was Sam's job to protect the school.

While Sam was walking home alone on Thursday, Mr. Nekobi's words echoed in his head: *"The school is planning something big. . . ."*

What could the school — Sam's thoughts were interrupted by the feeling of cold fingers on his back.

"Eek!" Sam shrieked. He spun around. "Lucy! You scared me!"

"Did you think it was the school trying to eat you?" Lucy teased. "I don't know what you and Antonio have been doing the past three days, but you'd better be ready for tomorrow."

"What's tomorrow?" Sam asked.

Lucy rolled her eyes. Then she shoved a crumpled-up piece of paper into Sam's hands.

As Sam read the words, his heart began to pound. It all made sense. Sam knew exactly when the school would strike!

BEAST FROM BELOW

12

It was opening night, and the school auditorium was packed.

Sam stuck his head through the red curtains and peered out. He saw hundreds of parents and teachers in the audience. He even saw his mom, and Lucy's little brother.

Students were changing into their costumes backstage. Antonio, as Peter Pan, was wearing green from head to toe. And Lucy wore a yellow dress as Wendy.

Sam pulled Antonio aside. "I've got a feeling something *really* bad is going to happen," he whispered. "Maybe we should stop the play. We could tell Ms. Grinker —"

Antonio cut him off. "Sam, everyone will think we're crazy. *I'm* still not sure we aren't."

Sam sighed. He knew Antonio was right.

"Besides," Antonio said, "I've got my lucky peanut butter and jelly sandwich in my pocket! What could go wrong?"

Sam rolled his eyes. "Lucky sandwich . . ."

Before Sam could say anything else, the lights dimmed. The audience went quiet. The play was about to start.

Lucy rushed over. She pulled Antonio toward the stage. "Wish us luck, Sam!" she whispered as she and Antonio marched out onstage.

Sam sighed. "Good luck. . . ."

Two hours later, Sam was smiling from ear to ear — he couldn't believe it: The play was actually going okay! Lucy was saying her lines perfectly, Antonio made an *awesome* Peter Pan, and the audience was clapping *a ton*.

Maybe he had been worried for nothing.

The next scene was the most exciting part of the play: the big finish. Antonio and Lucy were strung up on wires high above the stage like they were flying.

"Sam!" Ms. Grinker said. "It's your turn onstage!"

"Oh, right," Sam muttered.

He stepped out into the spotlight and began to say his lines: "I am Noodler, Captain Hook's friendly pirate. And I order you to —"

Sam stopped. He felt something move below his feet. . . .

With horror, Sam realized the school had been *waiting for him*. Now that *he* was onstage, the school was coming to life!

This was it.

There were some whispers in the audience. People thought Sam had forgotten his lines.

But Sam didn't *care* about his lines.

He cared about what he saw next:

A trapdoor in the floor
was opening!

From up high, Lucy and Antonio saw it, too.

The trapdoor was opening wider and wider. It was like the wooden stage was suddenly made of rubber.

Sam's heart pounded as he looked down into the darkness below. There, he saw the true terror. . . .

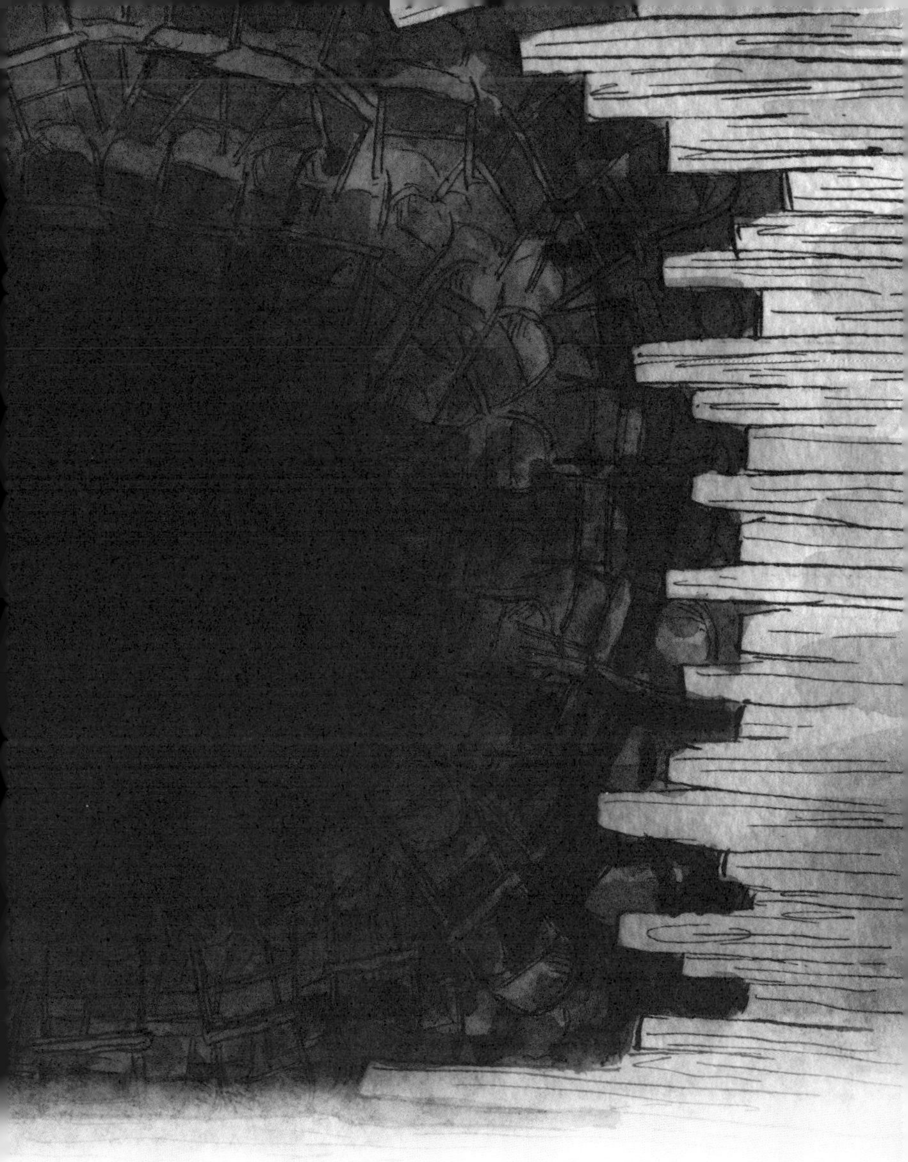

Beneath the stage, hundreds of metal folding chairs were opening and closing like a set of giant jagged teeth!

And high above this hungry mouth, Antonio and Lucy were dangling on their wires. They were about to be eaten alive!

CHOMP!

CHOMP!

CHOMP!

WORM MOUTH

13

SWISSHH!!

The big red curtains swooshed shut. The audience gasped. They could no longer see the stage.

A closet door banged open behind Sam. Then the floorboards lifted up to form a slide. Ms. Grinker and the other students tumbled backward into the closet.

From offstage, Mr. Nekobi yelled, "Sam! It's happening!" He ran toward Sam. But the curtain ropes grabbed hold of him. The ropes flung Mr. Nekobi inside the closet, too. The door snapped shut.

Next, the lights went out. Only one spotlight stayed on. It was pointed at Sam, Lucy, and Antonio.

The audience can't see the stage, and the teachers and students are trapped in the closet! Sam thought. *I'm the only one who can save everyone!*

The chair mouth began
to climb up out of its
hole in the floor —
like a worm
coming up out of
the ground!

Lucy and Antonio began kicking and screaming. "What is that?!" Lucy yelled.

Antonio thrashed on his wire, trying to get away from the huge teeth. As he swung, his lucky peanut butter and jelly sandwich slipped from his pocket. It fell down into the giant mouth. The sandwich splattered against the chair teeth.

Sam got an idea.

"I'll be back!" he shouted up to his friends.

"Don't leave us, Sam!" Lucy cried. She was fiddling with her wire, trying to untie herself.

"Just trust me," Sam said. He leapt over the giant mouth.

Everyone in the audience gasped as Sam jumped out from behind the closed curtain. He sprinted out of the dark auditorium and into the hallway.

When Sam reached the end of the hall, he pushed open the lunchroom door. It was quiet and dark, but as soon as Sam stepped inside, the lunchroom *came alive*. The chairs shook. The long tables buckled up and down, and the ceiling lamps swung.

A deep moaning sound came from a speaker on the wall. Eerie Elementary was howling.

MMMUURRRRGHHHHHHHH!!

Sam needed to get into the kitchen, but every step he took seemed to make the school angrier. Packages of cookies exploded. Tables flipped over. Light bulbs above his head shattered!

Suddenly, the vending machine began firing bottles of water at him. One blasted Sam in the chest, knocking him onto his back.

I'll never make it all the way to the kitchen, he thought. *Unless . . .*

Sam thought back to his training. He remembered Antonio telling him to use what was around him.

Sam leapt to his feet, grabbed an orange lunch tray, and held it over his chest. He hopped up on a table and sprinted down the length of it! As he charged toward the kitchen, the vending machine fired more water bottles at him.

The bottles bounced off his shield.

Sam jumped off the end of the table, hit the ground, and rolled into the kitchen.

Then he saw it: the one thing that could save his friends.

EAT THIS!

14

Sam stared up at a giant drum of peanut butter. It was stacked high atop a table full of food supplies. He shook the table, then jumped back. Jars of secret sauce and cans of soup crashed to the ground — along with the peanut butter drum.

SUPE
SIZE
PEANUT
BUTTER
TOMA
PAST
POTA
Secret
Sauce

Sam rolled the drum out through the lunchroom door. He gave it a heavy push. It barreled down the hall, clearing a path.

POW! The drum knocked a monstrous chair out of the way.

BOOM! The drum sent a spinning trash can flying.

KLAM! KLAM! KLAM! The drum blasted

through a set of locker doors.

The peanut butter drum crushed everything in its way!

At last, Sam made it backstage with the drum. Lucy ran toward him.

"Lucy!" Sam yelled. "How'd you get down?"

"I was able to untie myself. But I couldn't reach Antonio. He's still stuck and —"

Sam pushed the drum toward the stage and looked up. The giant mouth had grown larger! It was now made of *hundreds* of folding chairs that together formed a hundred teeth. Two of the teeth had hold of Antonio's green pants. Any second now, he would be eaten alive!

"HELP!" yelled Antonio.

"Sam, what can we do?" asked Lucy.

"Follow my lead," Sam said.

The mouth was about to chomp into Antonio. Just then, Sam shouted, "Hey, Eerie Elementary! Are you hungry?"

The monstrous chair mouth turned away from Antonio. It faced Sam and Lucy and let out a growl.

Sam and Lucy didn't flinch. They stood perfectly still.

The mouth opened wider.

Lucy grabbed hold of Sam's arm. Sam held his breath.

As the giant mouth charged toward them, the stage floorboards were breaking apart. Sam stared into the center of the chomping, thrashing mouth. It was upon them.

"NOW!" Sam screamed.

Together, Sam and Lucy kicked the heavy peanut butter drum as hard as they could.

It bowled across the stage, right into the giant mouth! The teeth chomped down on the drum, and —

KA-BOOM!!!

SUPE

PE

The drum burst open, and gallons of peanut butter flew everywhere. The peanut butter was gumming up the monster's mouth. The chewing slowed, then stopped.

Lucy and Sam bumped fists.

"You did it!" Antonio shouted from up high.

"I couldn't have done it without you two!" said Sam, smiling.

The sticky mouth slipped back down through the trapdoor. The trapdoor closed.

The floor returned to normal.

It was over.

Eerie Elementary was silent.

Then — *all of the sudden* — the stage curtains swooshed open!

SAM GRAVES, HALL MONITOR

15

The lights came on. The closet door opened. Ms. Grinker, Mr. Nekobi, and the students stumbled out.

For a moment, everyone was quiet. The audience looked around, confused.

Ms. Grinker walked out onstage. “Um . . . well, uh . . . Let’s have a hand for the kids! That play was amazing!” she said.

Sam's mom started clapping. "Wonderful job, Sam!" she yelled.

Soon, everyone was clapping. No one had any idea what had just happened.

Lucy helped Antonio down from his wire. Then she whispered to Sam, "Um, now what?"

Sam smiled. "Now we take our bow."

Backstage, the students were changing out of their costumes.

Mr. Nekobi took Sam aside. "You did well tonight, Sam Graves," he said. "Everyone here is in good hands." Then he walked away.

Sam ran over to his friends. He burst out, "I told you guys the school was alive! Now do you believe me?"

Antonio and Lucy were talking so fast that Sam could hardly understand them. He laughed and said, "Guys, relax. I'll tell you *everything*."

And he did. As they were waiting out front for their parents, Sam told his friends everything there was to tell about Eerie Elementary.

The school cast long shadows, lit by the moon. Two large windows were open, and inside two lights burned like eyes, watching the three best friends.

EERIE

1923
SCHOOL

Sam reached into his backpack. He felt the hall monitor sash that, just a few days earlier, he had been embarrassed to wear. Now he had a sudden urge to put it on. He knew it wouldn't be long before Eerie Elementary would strike again. . . .

Jack Chabert was a hall monitor at Joshua Eaton Elementary School in Reading, Massachusetts. But unlike our hero Sam Graves's school, Jack's school was not alive. Jack's life as a hall monitor was much less exciting than Sam's — and not nearly as scary!

Today, Jack Chabert monitors the halls of a different building: a strange, old apartment building in New York City that he calls home. His days are spent playing video games, eating junk food, and reading comic books. And at night, he walks the halls, always prepared for the moment when his building will come alive.

Sam Ricks went to a haunted grade school, but he never got to be the hall monitor. And, as far as he knows, the school never tried to eat him. Sam graduated from the University of Baltimore with a master's degree in design. He teaches illustration and design at The Art Institute of Salt Lake City, Utah. And he illustrates strange tales from the comfort of his nearby, non-carnivorous home.

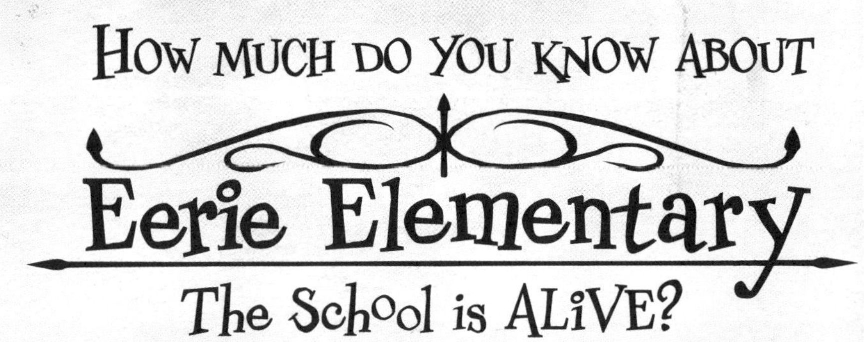

HOW MUCH DO YOU KNOW ABOUT Eerie Elementary

The School is ALIVE?

Quicksand is a **compound word**. A compound word is made up of two words that come together to make one new word. What is quicksand? Use what you know about **quick** and **sand** to figure out the meaning.

Who is Mr. Nekobi? And how does he help Sam?

Look at the picture on page 54. What is Sam doing?

How does Antonio's sandwich help Sam save everyone?

Would **you** want to be the hall monitor? Use examples from the book to write **why** or **why not.**